The Four-Legged Ghosts

The Four-Legged Ghosts

MARY HOFFMAN

PICTURES BY

LAURA L. SEELEY

Dial Books for Young Readers *New York*

For Cody Seets, my "Favorite Fan"
–M.H.

For Mom and Dad
–L.L.S.

First published in the United States 1993
by Dial Books for Young Readers
A Division of Penguin Books USA Inc.
375 Hudson Street · New York, New York 10014
Published in Great Britain 1992
by Orchard Books as *The Ghost Menagerie*
Text copyright © 1992 by Mary Hoffman
Pictures copyright © 1993 by Laura L. Seeley
Designed by Heather Wood
All rights reserved
Printed in the U.S.A.
First Edition
1 3 5 7 9 10 8 6 4 2

Library of Congress Cataloging in Publication Data
Hoffman, Mary, 1945–
[The ghost menagerie]
The four-legged ghosts / Mary Hoffman
illustrated by Laura L. Seeley.—1st ed.
p.   cm.
Previously published as : The ghost menagerie.
Summary : Despite Carrie's asthma, her parents
present brother Alex with a pet mouse, but the mouse has
magic powers and creates havoc by summoning up the ghosts
of all the animals that have ever lived in the house.
ISBN 0-8037-1466-1 (trade)—ISBN 0-8037-1645-1 (library)
[1. Animal ghosts—Fiction. 2. Ghosts—Fiction.
3. Magic—Fiction. 4. Mice—Fiction. 5. Pets—Fiction.
6. Asthma—Fiction.] I. Seeley, Laura L., ill. II. Title.
PZ7.H67562Fo   1993   [Fic]—dc20   93-12591   CIP   AC

Contents

1

Starting Small

Alex Brodie had tried really hard to hate his sister, but he had to give it up. Other boys had younger sisters who were a real pain, but Carrie wasn't. Even though it was her fault that the Brodies couldn't have pets. Well, not exactly her fault; Carrie couldn't help having asthma, which was set off by dust or fur or hair. The trouble was Carrie was really nice, and she was as sorry as he was about the pets. They both loved animals.

When Carrie was born, Alex's parents had bought him a kitten as a sort of consolation prize. Then the baby started wheezing, and the doctor said the kitten had to go. Alex could just remember holding a purring bundle of ginger fur.

But Carrie had cried so much when she had been old enough to understand this story that he couldn't even hold that against her.

And it wasn't as if Marmalade had been taken to the pound. He had gone to old Mrs. Grieves, a few doors down Ferry Road, and had grown very stout. He still let Alex tickle his ears on the way past Mrs. Grieves's front yard but never showed any signs of missing him.

Alex sighed. It would be nice to have a cat to sit on your lap while you did your homework. Or a dog you could take for a walk instead of doing your homework. Even a hamster would be some fun; you could teach it tricks.

But it was no good; they were all too furry.

Yet when Alex had pointed out that pythons and boa constrictors weren't furry at all, his mother had vetoed even this sensible suggestion.

She was probably right though, thought Alex gloomily. Large snakes might not be furry, but their food would be. He didn't want Carrie to be the first child to get an asthma attack from someone's dinner.

Alex doodled in his homework book, drawing a tiny dragon curled up in a dog basket, and wondered what Carrie and his parents were up to. They had gone off after school on a highly secret expedition, with lots of shushing and giggling.

He supposed it was to do with his eleventh birthday tomorrow. It was a lucky year: His birthday fell on a Saturday, and he was having a party. Not a Jell-O and ice-cream and silly games kind, but a grown-up meal out at McDonald's with Carrie and his five best friends, followed by a downtown movie.

Just then the front door banged, and there was a lot more whispering and chattering in the hall. Alex resolutely continued with his drawing, even though he was dying of curiosity. He knew from experience that surprises were best if they stayed surprises. There was a knock on his door.

"Can I come in?" called Carrie, and burst in without waiting for an answer. She was hugging herself to keep the secret in, and shining like a Christmas tree.

"What are you doing?" she asked, looking at Alex's picture.

"Inventing a pet for us," said Alex. "A nonsneezable, unwheezeable, strokable, cuddly little dragon."

"Oh, wouldn't it be great?" said Carrie, curling up on Alex's bed with the dragon picture in her hand. "What should we call him?"

"Cedric," said Alex immediately, without knowing why. The name just seemed to come to him, and with it a funny sort of tingling in his scalp. He shook his head and thought how useful it would be to have a pet dragon; you could aim it at people you didn't like. You'd probably only need to do it once.

⌣

The next morning Alex woke with the special warm feeling he had only on birthdays and Christmas Day. He yawned and snuggled under the covers, enjoying the Saturdayness of not having to get dressed before breakfast, and looking forward to his presents.

There they were, after breakfast, a satisfying heap of lumpy shapes in bright paper, and in the middle a large something that gave off a strange ting and rattle every now and then through its untidy wrappings. Alex left that one until last. As he pulled off the paper, the tinging got louder.

"It's a mouse!" shouted Carrie, dancing

around the room, unable to contain her joy any longer.

There in the middle of the coffee table was a shiny-bright new cage and in it a small but active white mouse.

"I don't understand," stammered Alex. "How come? I mean, won't it . . . ?"

"No," said his mother. "We've already checked with Doctor Murdoch, and he said that since Carrie is so much better, one small mouse shouldn't cause any problems. Of course, you'll have to keep him in your room."

Alex didn't mind that. He couldn't believe it—his own pet at last! It didn't matter that the mouse was only about two inches long, if you didn't count the tail. He was very intelligent-looking and lively. Alex put his finger through the bars and the mouse promptly bit it.

"It's all right," said his father. "The pet shop man says he'll soon get used to you and let you handle him. You just have to let him get to know you."

"What will you call him?" asked Carrie.

"I think I'll call him Cedric, same as our dragon," Alex replied thoughtfully, and the same tingly feeling lifted his hair as when he had named the dragon. He sucked his finger, and wondered if the mouse could be trained to bite enemies.

Alex and Carrie spent the rest of the day installing Cedric in his new home and training him to let them stroke him. Within a few hours he knew the smell of their fingers and stopped trying to bite them. Carrie didn't sneeze once.

"I wonder if he'll be lonely without any other mice," she said.

"He's got us, hasn't he?" said Alex, pouring Cedric from one hand to another, like milk from a jug.

"Yes and we've got him. I mean *you* have," Carrie heroically corrected herself.

"You can share him," said Alex, feeling very noble.

"It's great, isn't it?" said Carrie happily, stroking Cedric's back with one finger.

And then she and Alex said at the same time, "But I wish we could have lots of animals."

Afterward, when all the trouble started and they looked back on this moment, they thought they should have felt some sort of electric shock, or that the mouse should have emitted a weird Spielberg-blue light. But at the time they just laughed and said, "Jinx!" and put Cedric back in his cage, quite unaware that their lives were about to change spectacularly.

Cedric Whitgift Blanco the fifty-seventh looked through the bars of his latest cage, while his new owners went off to get "washed for McDonald," whom he assumed was their clan chief. His bright raspberry eyes took in every detail of his surroundings. The posters of long-haired men with guitars did not mean much to him, but the high moulded ceiling and plaster roses around the light fixture stirred memories in his mouse blood that were not his. He felt as if he had been in this house before. As soon as he had come into the house, he had said in his head *Cedric is back!*, which was why Alex had come up with the right name even though he had wasted it on a paper dragon first.

Cedric (WB 57th) was no ordinary mouse. He understood human speech for a start. He was not just unusual; he was very clever. Now he jogged slowly around on the wheel in his cage, thinking over all he had heard in the Brodie household so far. He liked what he had seen of it. Two loving children and no cats added up to a good home for a mouse. He felt sorry for the children that they couldn't have as many animals as they wanted, though for himself he was quite satisfied not to share lodgings with a cat or dog.

I wonder? thought Cedric, stepping suddenly off the wheel and sitting down to polish his long whiskers with his front paws. The feeling, deep in his blood, that his family had some connection with this house gave him an idea. There *was* a kind of animal that he could share his new home with that wouldn't make Carrie sneeze. It was a simple enough job for a mouse like him to arrange—but perhaps he should start in a small way, so as not to alarm the children, get them used to the idea gradually. He could always move on to bigger things later. Anyway, being in this house made him think of his ancestors. Cedric curled up in his shredded paper and concentrated on his grandfather, Cedric Whitgift Blanco the fifty-fifth.

⌣

When Alex came back from the movies, full
of popcorn and chocolate raisins—some of
which he had saved as a treat for Cedric—
he went to say good night to his very own
pet. And curled up in the colored loops and
coils of paper he saw not one small white
mouse, but two.

2

Batty

That night Alex couldn't sleep. He kept getting up to count his mouse. The answer was two every time. Eventually he fell into an exhausted sleep as the light came in through his curtains, but he was soon woken up by his mother calling that breakfast was ready.

Sunday breakfast in the Brodie household was a ritual. It was very late, to allow everyone the luxury of not getting up in a rush, and never happened until the parents had read the Sunday paper in bed with a pot of coffee. Normally Alex was awake long before being called and could smell the pancakes his father always made as part of the special routine.

Unfortunately the leisurely Sunday breakfast was also the usual time for family conversation, when the parents actually listened to the children's answers to their questions. It was the worst time for Alex's mother to ask, "And how is your mouse this morning?" "Double," didn't seem an appropriate reply, but Alex couldn't think how he was going to keep this incomprehensible piece of information to himself. He longed for breakfast to be over so he could let Carrie in on the secret.

Fortunately Dad was anxious to get on with the attic remodeling, which was in its last stages now. So Alex was able to escape, dragging Carrie with him. As soon as they were in his room, he pointed dramatically to the cage, and his sister gave a satisfying gasp of amazement.

"Oh, Alex, how sweet! Cedric must be a

girl after all—she must have had a baby in the night!"

Alex rolled his eyes heavenward.

"Don't be such a deadbrain, Carrie! This mouse is the same size as Cedric. And even if it weren't, mice have whole litters of babies, not just one at a time."

"But then how did it get here?" Carrie asked reasonably.

"The only explanation I can think of is that there must have been a second mouse in the cage all the time, hiding in the bedding or something."

Carrie looked doubtful. At that moment their mother breezed in with that light knock she gave for politeness' sake, but never waited for a response to. Okay, thought Alex, this is where we find out whether I'm allowed to keep them both.

She put Alex's clean laundry on his bed, then came over to the cage. Alex and Carrie both held their breath.

"You know, he really is an intelligent-looking animal," she said, staring straight at both mice.

An eerie feeling crept along Alex's spine. *His mother could not see the second mouse!* After she left, he looked at Carrie. If his sister hadn't noticed the two mice right away, Alex would by now have been convinced that he was losing his marbles.

Carrie's mouth was slightly open and her eyes were round. They both looked hard again at the two mice. There was no doubt which one was Cedric. The other one was just as solid-looking, but there was *something* about it, something that made it look more like an example of a mouse than an actual individual one. Gingerly Alex opened the cage door and took the intruder into his cupped hands. He could feel it all right, but at the same time he had an icy and immediate conviction that it was not really there. Wordlessly he handed it to Carrie, who obviously felt the same thing.

They put the second mouse back as Cedric

watched them with his bright inquiring look. I think they're pleased, but they haven't really understood yet, he mused mousefully. Time to extend the experiment. But slowly does it. His whiskers twitched, and his mind reached back into the years to make contact with other creatures who had lived in this house.

Alex and Carrie were by now out in the hallway. Carrie had her fist stuffed into her mouth as if to prevent a scream from escaping.

"You two busy?" called Dad from up at the top of the house. "I could do with a hand up here."

They couldn't think of a reason to say no, so they climbed the ladder into the attic. It was nearly finished. It had always been tall enough to stand up in, and Dad had put two big windows in the sloping roof so that it was quite light and airy. Alex had hoped passionately that he would be allowed to have it for his own bedroom, but Mom and

Dad said they were getting a boarder; it would help with the cost of the remodeling. Alex had always felt there was a flaw in their logic somewhere, but he couldn't quite put his finger on it.

It was all plastered and painted now and Dad was laying a piece of green carpet. The boarder was supposed to be moving in the next week, and there was still the job of getting some furniture up the ladder.

"Ah, good, there you are," said Dad, and as he turned around to show them what he wanted, Alex and Carrie both saw the bats. They were tiny pig-faced black mice with leathery little wings like miniature umbrellas. And there were at least fifty of them. The ones that were asleep were just hanging peacefully upside down along the ribs of the roof. But about a dozen, disturbed by Dad's activity, had alighted on his shoulders and on his head. Furry, inquisitive faces peered into his, and he was obviously quite unaware of them.

Even though Alex knew this must be the same sort of phenomenon as the extra mouse, he couldn't help himself. His voice came out as high and squeaky as any bat could wish. "Dad, be careful, you might hurt one."

"One what?" Dad inquired, brushing vaguely at his shoulder as if he had a cobweb on it.

"Oh!" cried Carrie, dashing forward to catch a little bat who had been knocked off. "You must stop doing the attic, Dad. They're a protected species."

"Yes," said Alex. "I think you're supposed to call the humane society if you find a colony of them."

Dad looked from one to the other in bewilderment and then broke into a big grin. He was quite easygoing as dads go.

"I get it," he said, "bats in the belfry. Okay, now the joke is over. I want you two to help me unroll this piece of carpet so that it's straight."

Alex gave Carrie a nudge and they some-how managed to do what they had to, without mentioning the bats again. But all the time they were in the attic, the air was full of awakened flitter mice, squeaking and flapping around their heads. When Dad went down to get some more nails, Alex caught one gently and felt the same cold certainty that it was from another dimension.

Carrie watched his face. "What does it mean, Alex?" she asked. There had never yet been anything that Alex had not been able to explain to the satisfaction of his kid sister.

"Tell you later," he whispered as they heard Dad coming back up the ladder.

They sat through their late lunch in si-lence, while their parents talked about day-beds and night tables. As soon as the meal was over, the children went out into the yard. By unspoken agreement they were not ready to face the mice again yet. As they wandered down to the end of the lawn,

Carrie spotted something moving slowly in the flower bed. It was a large tortoise.

"Oh, look," she said. "It must have escaped from someone's yard. They're very rare now, aren't they?"

"Hang on a minute," said Alex. "Try touching it."

"You don't think it's another . . ." Slowly Carrie bent down and picked up the tortoise. Its ancient eyes looked at them solemnly, and it moved its wrinkled neck from side to side. Carrie almost dropped it. She turned huge frightened eyes to Alex. "What does it mean?" she asked again. "Why don't they feel like ordinary animals?"

"I don't know," said Alex, "but I think I can guess who does. We've got to find out about that second mouse. Come on."

They ran indoors and up to Alex's room, taking the stairs two at a time.

In the cage both Cedrics waited. "Now look here, Cedric," said Alex firmly.

Both mice looked up expectantly at their name, but Alex wasn't deceived.

"I mean the real one," he said. One of the Cedrics looked away embarrassed. The other returned Alex's stare beadily. "You're behind all this, aren't you? First a second mouse, then bats, and now a tortoise. Only they aren't real animals; they just look like them. What exactly are they?"

The mouse blinked once, then spoke:

"Well, actually, they're ghosts."

3

Rabbiting On

It hadn't seemed at all strange to either Alex or Carrie that Cedric could talk. When you considered the other things he could do, that was the least marvel. When they had gotten over their shock about the second mouse being a ghost, Cedric had formally introduced them to his grandfather.

"So, you've seen the bats and the tortoise?" said Cedric casually. He was proud that his plan was working.

"Yes, we have," said Alex.

"Are they *all* ghosts?" asked Carrie.

"They are," said Cedric. "Of animals who

used to live in this house—or its garden."

"But how do you do it?" asked Alex. "Can you bring back the ghost of any animal?"

"Could you do a cat?" asked Carrie eagerly. "I've always wanted a cat. But they're too furry—they would make me sneeze."

"That's why I summoned the ghosts, my dear," said Cedric. "I heard you talking about the sneezing problem. But are you sure about a cat? I can never see the point of them myself."

"But *how* can you summon ghosts?" Alex persisted, interrupting him. "I mean, what sort of a mouse are you?"

Cedric had drawn himself up to his full two inches to announce, "I am the seventeenth son of a seventeenth son."

"Wow!" said Carrie.

"What does that mean?" asked Alex.

"It means," said Cedric importantly, "magic."

"You'll be late for school!" yelled Alex's mom as he hauled himself blearily out of bed after another restless night. This time it had been excitement keeping him awake. His whole life had changed in two days. Not only did he have a pet mouse (two, if you counted Cedric Senior), he had his own personal miracle worker and a growing collection of animal ghosts. He looked out the window and saw that the backyard was full of rabbits. He called to Carrie and they both got dressed quickly and slipped outside.

"Oh," said Carrie, picking up a brown rabbit. "Aren't they adorable? If he can do this, surely he can do a cat."

"I don't know," said Alex. "A cat might not be such a good idea."

"Why not?" said Carrie. "Look!" She buried her face in the soft furry ears of the rabbit and came up smiling and sneeze-free.

"I didn't mean from your point of view," said Alex. "I was thinking of the Cedrics. I

definitely got the impression that our Cedric was anti-cat."

"But it's not as if a ghost cat could hurt them, is it?" said Carrie.

"Isn't it?" said Alex. "We don't really know *what* they can do, do we?"

But they were about to find out. At breakfast the bread had a chewed corner, but the crumbs were all still there. "Has that mouse of yours escaped?" Dad asked Alex. But Mom said she had seen a brown house mouse skittering away behind the stove. They began to talk about traps.

Carrie and Alex exchanged horrified glances. "It's all right," Alex whispered to her, "you can't kill a ghost—they're already dead." But he didn't feel altogether sure of this himself.

He would have loved to take Cedric, the real one, to school but Mom gave that idea a firm no. So Alex had to content himself with describing his new pet to his best friend, Rusty Murray.

"He's great, Rusty," said Alex, "really magic."

"Oh, yeah?" said Rusty, interested. "Can he do tricks and stuff?"

Alex nodded. "He can do tricks that would earn him a fortune on television."

"This I've got to see," said Rusty. "I'll come back after school, okay?"

Alex didn't know what to say. He didn't know how to tell Rusty that when he had said "magic" he really *meant* magic, but he couldn't think of any reason to put his friend off from coming to see Cedric.

So after school they met Carrie and headed for the bus. "Rusty wants to see Cedric," Alex told Carrie, putting a finger to his lips to indicate that she wasn't to say anything about the other animals in their home. Carrie nodded. She was beginning to think she had imagined them all anyway.

When they arrived home, Mrs. Brodie was in a dither. "First it's mice in the kitchen," she said. "Now something's gone and chewed all Dad's lettuces in the vegetable garden." Alex and Carrie guiltily remembered their rabbits. Dad was very proud of growing all their own green stuff, as well as doing a full-time job and all their own house repairs. He wasn't going to be happy about the lettuces.

They took Rusty upstairs to Alex's room.

"Hey, you didn't say you had two of them," said Rusty the minute he looked in the cage.

"Good afternoon," said Cedric, "I can see you are another very intelligent human being."

Rusty sat down hard and suddenly on Alex's bed and passed a hand over his forehead, pale now under its sprinkling of gold freckles. Alex and Carrie were almost as surprised as he was.

"You can see Cedric too?" asked Carrie.

"See him?" said Rusty. "I think I just heard him."

"No," said Alex. "Not him—she means

the other one. They're both called Cedric."

Poor Rusty. He had been under the impression that at least one of the mice was a regular rodent, and it took some time to explain it all. Both Alex and Carrie felt strangely relieved that another person could see the ghost mouse, and as soon as Rusty was up to it, they took him to meet the other animals.

Out in the garden, Mom was shaking her head sadly over Dad's lettuces. "I can't imagine what's been doing it," she said, staring straight at the tortoise taking huge bites out of the lower leaves, while a young rabbit nibbled his way to the sweet heart of the plant.

Rusty stared fascinated at Mom. "Can't she see them?" he whispered. When Mom had gone back in, Carrie picked up the floppy rabbit.

"Have you noticed they don't actually eat any of it?" she said.

"Why doesn't your magic mouse bring

back the ghosts of their hutches and cages?" asked Rusty. "If this sort of thing goes on, your parents are bound to get suspicious."

They went to have a word with Cedric about this, but he was quite indignant.

"Isn't it bad enough that they were caged and imprisoned in their lives?" he said. "Do you want me to trap and confine their spirits as well?"

Alex felt very uncomfortable. "Do you hate your cage so much?" he asked Cedric.

Cedric gave a contemptuous twitch of his whiskers. "Do you think we are staying in here because of that puny little catch?" He flexed his paws and woffled his nose at the cage door. All three children saw the metal latch spring back and the door swing open. Cedric strolled out, nudging his grandfather to come too.

"Oh, don't be offended," pleaded Carrie. "We didn't know you were so unhappy. And Mom says you *have* to keep small animals in cages."

Cedric turned back and went into the cage, closing the door behind him with a flick of his long pink tail.

Later that evening, Alex couldn't find Carrie. Eventually he tracked her down at the edge of the backyard, where she sat in the fading light, cradling a little rabbit in her arms and crying her heart out.

"What's the matter?" he asked.

"This one's a baby," she said between sobs. "It means it must have been only a baby when it died."

Alex hadn't thought of that. It was really sad if you started to think that all these animals had died.

"But look, Carrie," he said gently, taking the rabbit out of her arms. "It's not as if he's *going* to die. Whatever happened is already over and done with. It happened years ago. And he *looks* perfectly all right. He even seems happy."

Alex stroked the rabbit's ears and tickled his tummy. Gradually Carrie cheered up.

"I am worried about the rabbits though," said Alex. "I mean, how many do you think there are?"

"About fifteen, counting the baby ones," said Carrie.

"Well, do you think that's all? And is Cedric going to stop at mice and rabbits? There's going to be a lot of trouble if any more plants get damaged, and I reckon we'll somehow end up getting the blame."

They went back to the house in a thoughtful mood. They had always been told what a responsibility it was to keep a pet, but they had never really understood it until now. Mom took one look at Carrie, whose eyes were red and swollen from crying, and sent her straight to bed, thinking her asthma was acting up.

Alex fell into a deep sleep the moment his head crashed onto the pillow. But he was woken up soon afterward by someone shaking his shoulder. It was Carrie, trembling with excitement. "Come and see!" was all she would say.

Alex stumbled along to his sister's room and looked in. On her quilt, curled up as comfortably as only a cat can be, was a beautiful long-haired calico. Alex left Carrie snuggled down in bed with her arm around the purring cat, an expression of perfect bliss on her face.

"Thanks, Cedric," yawned Alex as he crawled back into bed, "you're a mouse in a million."

4

Beauty Is in the Eye of the Beholder

"I can't understand it," Mom was saying to Dad. "Last night she looked as if she was in for a really bad asthma attack, and this morning she's just fine."

Alex smiled. If only his parents knew it was a cat bringing Carrie such good health! But it was true. She was looking better this morning than she had been for months. Alex on the other hand was beginning to feel distinctly peaked. All these broken nights were doing him no good at all. Carrie was so happy sitting there at breakfast with the glamorous calico cat (who had informed them her name was Beauty) lying on her lap. The only problem was remembering not to stroke the cat while her parents were looking. They might think it was a little odd to stroke something that wasn't there.

It was with great difficulty that Alex got Carrie out the door and off to school without the cat.

"But why can't I?" pleaded Carrie. "No one would know but me."

"Wouldn't they?" said Alex. "Remember that Rusty could see all the animals. I bet it's only grown-ups that can't."

Alex had a hunch that it would mean trouble if they tried to take any of the ghost animals away from their proper home. But it did make the school day seem agonizingly long. He couldn't wait to see what Cedric would produce next. When they did return home, with Rusty in tow again, all they could see was furniture. The hall was crowded with bits and pieces—some new, some secondhand—that were going to furnish the attic. Dad was carrying a plastic-wrapped mattress up the stairs. Beauty dashed down between his feet to welcome Carrie, and though Dad couldn't see her, he tripped and cursed just the same as if he had.

Rusty looked startled.

"Don't say anything about the cat," hissed Alex. "Remember Dad can't see her."

"And don't mention the black-and-white kitten either," giggled Carrie in a whisper.

"What black-and-white kitten?" Alex demanded.

"That one," said Carrie, pointing to the living room windowsill, where a small cat sat washing herself.

"What about the tabby?" grinned Rusty. "Can I mention that?"

"Tabby?" said Carrie.

Rusty pointed. There was indeed a tabby, just behind them on the doormat, which had not been there when they came in. Rusty whistled long and low.

"That Cedric's really pulling out all the stops, isn't he? I mean when he does cats, he really does cats!"

Mom's voice floated down the stairs, sounding muffled. "Can you kids play outside for a while? We've got to get the room ready for the magician who's moving in tomorrow." At least it sounded as if that was what she had said.

The children looked at one another.

"Wow!" said Rusty. "I wonder if it's anyone famous."

Alex shrugged. "It can be one with a pointy hat and a wand, as far as I'm concerned," he said. "After all, we've already got a mouse with supernatural powers and a whole houseful of ghost pets. Why not a magician in the attic? The more the merrier."

"Come on," said Carrie, "let's take the cats out to the backyard."

They each scooped up a purring puss. The three cats had a wonderful time stalking rabbits, chasing butterflies, and scampering, bushy-tailed, up trees. Beauty rolled on her back on the lawn, exposing her creamy white belly fur. She turned her head upside down and rubbed her ears ecstatically on the grass, making little chirruping, crooning noises. If you hadn't known she was a ghost, you'd have said she was glad to be alive.

Just then Big Tam arrived. He was the Terminator of Ferry Road, battle-scarred, notch-eared, and enormous. He was a brown tabby, of the same general build and personality as a yearling tiger. Big Tam sat on the fence and twitched his long thick tail. In his few years of life on Ferry Road, Big Tam had won more fights and sired more kittens than any other tomcat. But he had never set eyes on a cat like Beauty. She had class. Big Tam yowled and Beauty looked up at him. She meowed coyly. The children watched, fascinated. They all had a feeling that Big Tam was in for a disappointment this time, but they didn't know how it was going to come about.

As the big tabby flowed down from the fence and advanced toward Beauty, he suddenly found himself nose to nose with two enormous Irish wolfhounds, who had not been there a moment before. Nothing in Big Tam's life in a quiet suburb had prepared him for such an experience. He underwent the cat equivalent of a serious nervous breakdown in about thirty seconds. Alex later swore that some of Big Tam's stripes turned white. The toughest cat on the block turned tail and bolted out of the yard, with two ghostly hounds barking after him.

Beauty looked a little put out; she had been enjoying herself. She hissed at the dogs and walked stiffly back into the house. The children were enraptured by the great hairy hounds with their lolloping red tongues.

"Pleased to meet you," said one, with a strong Irish accent. "I'm Seamus and this is me old pal, Fergus."

"Top of the morning, I mean afternoon," said the other. "The Irish Guards, that's us.

That's what the old master used to call us."

"Get rid of anyone you don't want, we will," said Seamus.

"Like that mangy old tomcat," agreed Fergus. "Anyone else for us? How about a nice postman?"

"Haven't tasted postman for, oh, must be nigh on forty years," agreed Seamus.

The two dogs wandered around the yard, wagging their shaggy tails, while the children looked at one another in amazement. What *would* Cedric think of next?

"Sure, it's good to be back in the old place again, isn't it?" said Seamus.

"It is that, Seamus, boyo," agreed Fergus, scratching in the rose bed. "And I seem to remember burying a fine mutton bone somewhere around this spot—mind it must have been a fair while back."

"Stop!" cried Alex. "You mustn't dig there. Those are Dad's special roses."

The big dog stopped his digging and gave Alex an inquiring look.

"What do you think, Seamus, do I do what the young larrikin says?"

"Sure," said Seamus. "He must be the master here now. We'd better take our orders from him."

The two hounds obediently trotted at Alex's heels after that. But it was a little awkward when the children were called in for dinner and the Irish Guards insisted on accompanying them indoors. Rusty could hardly tear himself away to his own house, and he whispered fiercely to Alex, "I'll meet you outside school early tomorrow. Can't wait to hear what happens next."

"Well, that's that, then," said Dad, washing his hands at the sink and not noticing Seamus flopped out in front of the back door or Fergus lying under the table. "Mungo Mackindoe can come as soon as he wants. We're all ready for him."

"Who's that?" asked Alex, trying to find somewhere to put his feet.

"Don't you ever listen to anything that's said?" asked his mother. "Mr. Mackindoe is our new boarder. The one who's going to live upstairs."

"Oh, yes, the magician," said Alex sarcastically, his mouth full of potato.

"That's right," said Dad. "He's a lecturer up at the university. Quite a grand fellow."

"Amazing what you can get a degree in nowadays, isn't it?" whispered Alex to Carrie. But she wasn't really listening. She had her feet on Fergus's back, Beauty on her knee, and the black-and-white kitten on her shoulder. A magician was the last thing she needed at the moment.

5

A Magician
in the Attic

Mungo Mackindoe moved in the next afternoon. Normally, having a new member of the household would have been quite a big event in the lives of the Brodie children but as it was, they hardly noticed. He didn't look like a magician anyway. A first glance revealed a tallish, sandy-haired man in his forties, with glasses and a quiet voice. For Alex, who had spent the night half-pushed out of bed by two wolfhounds, he didn't rate a second look. Alex didn't expect to see much of the new boarder anyway. He wasn't going to have his meals with the family.

"Probably not a real magician at all," Alex told Carrie. "Probably just does card tricks."

They were in Alex's bedroom with the door safely locked against ghostly intruders. They had had no experience so far with any animals coming through walls. The two Cedrics were climbing all over them. Cedric the fifty-seventh had stopped halfway up Alex's arm at the word "magician." He had been feeling unsettled all evening.

"Who are you talking about?" he asked Alex.

"Our new boarder," said Alex. "Sandy-haired guy with whiskers. He's supposed to be a magician but he doesn't look like one."

Cedric gave the closest a mouse can get to a delicate cough. "Appearances can be deceptive, you know. Take me, for example."

"Yes," said Alex. "We wanted to talk to you about that. About your powers. Er, were you thinking of doing any more? I mean, we don't want to seem ungrateful and it's great having the dogs, but they were a little bit of a surprise."

"And they nearly dug up Dad's roses," added Carrie gently.

Cedric didn't answer for a while. Then he said, "There have been quite a lot of animals in this house over the years. Each time I concentrate and think about the past, I see more and more just waiting to come back. It seems a shame to tell them they can't."

Alex and Carrie looked at one another in silent horror. How many was "quite a lot?" They had visions of a house overrun with cats, dogs, parrots, and goodness knows what else that only they could see.

"Couldn't you just not concentrate and stop thinking back?" suggested Carrie.

Cedric looked embarrassed. "I can see you two don't understand the first thing about magic," he said huffily. "Now, please put Grandfather and me back in the cage; I have some thinking to do."

"I hope he didn't mean *that* kind of thinking," said Alex grimly, after they had put the mice back and gone to Carrie's room. Beauty was curled up in her usual favorite spot on the quilt. She started purring the minute she saw Carrie. But a moment later she swelled up to twice her normal size and started hissing, as a friendly spaniel emerged from under the bed.

"Oh, no," groaned Alex as Carrie caught the dog and put it firmly outside the door. "It *was* that kind of thinking!"

"Do you know what I think?" asked Carrie. "I think he doesn't know how to stop. I think he started with some sort of

spell and doesn't know how to switch it off."

Alex looked at her, appalled. "You mean he's going to go on until all the animals who have ever lived here have turned up? How old do you reckon this house is?"

"I don't know," shrugged Carrie. "Dad always says it's Victorian."

"Right. Well, what does that mean? Do you know?"

"No," said Carrie, "do you?"

"No," said Alex. "Let's look it up," and he took down an old encyclopedia from the bookshelf. After a moment he gasped. "Oh, no! It says here that 'Victorian' means 'during the reign of Queen Victoria in England.' And it also says she became queen in 1837! That's more than a hundred and fifty years ago. This house could have been here for a hundred and fifty years!"

"Why is that so bad?" asked Carrie.

"Just think of all the people who can live in a house in all that time! Some people only stay a year or two in one place. And just think of all the pets they could have had. Dogs and cats don't live anywhere near as long as humans, and little animals have very short lives—eighteen months is good going for a hamster."

Carrie didn't like this conversation. Nor did Beauty. The elegant cat yawned. "Well, I wasn't here a hundred years ago," she said. "My owner was a soldier in one of your silly wars."

"Which one?" asked Alex eagerly.

"I don't remember dates," said Beauty, beginning one of her elaborate washing rituals. "But he went around liberating places a long way from here—France was one, I think, and Italy was another."

"Oh," said Alex, disappointed. "That must have been the Second World War. So you lived here in the 1940s?"

"Possibly," said Beauty, losing interest.

"You see, Carrie, it all fits. The first animal to appear was Cedric's grandfather and mice don't live very long, so he can't have been from very long ago. If Beauty's from fifty years ago, that means Cedric's only gone about a half or a third of the way back. What I'm trying to say is, suppose he's planning to bring back every animal that has ever lived here for a century and a half? Fergus and Seamus take up too much room as it is, and who knows what I'll do if any more dogs decide to sleep on my bed."

Carrie still didn't see quite how serious the problem was.

"Not everyone who lived here would have had a pet," she said. "And some people live in the same place for years and years."

"But we still don't want more than we've got. I vote we go back to Cedric and tell him to stop. And I think we should, very politely, ask him to send back all the animals —apart from the Irish Guards and Beauty."

"And the black-and-white kitten," added Carrie quickly.

"Well, all right. But no more," said Alex.

"What about the rabbits?" asked Carrie.

"No," said Alex, "not the rabbits. Remember the lettuces."

"And we can't very well ask him to get rid of his own grandfather," Carrie continued.

"No-o," admitted Alex. "All right. The Irish Guards, Beauty, the black-and-white kitten, and Cedric the fifty-fifth. And that's final."

But it wasn't. When they got back to Alex's room, both Cedrics had vanished from their cage. The children searched everywhere for the mice. There was still no sign of them by bedtime, but Alex didn't want to tell their parents yet. He spent another restless night and ended up on the floor while Seamus and Fergus sprawled on his bed. All night long he imagined that other lonely ghost dogs scratched and whined at his door.

The next morning Dad was going to give them both a lift to school. There was no sign of Mungo Mackindoe. Alex followed Dad out of the kitchen, yawning and rubbing his eyes. The children waited on the corner while Dad opened the garage door and reversed the car carefully out into the road.

"Hop in," he said, opening the passenger doors. But the children just stood on the pavement staring into the garage.

"What's the matter with you two?" asked Dad. "I'll close it when I get back."

"No," said Alex, suddenly startled into life. "I'll do it now." He could not bear to see the sturdy piebald pony that was standing there harnessed to a carriage. Particularly since, up to two minutes ago, the garage had been full of blue Festiva.

By the time he got to school, Alex was thoroughly rattled. He cornered Rusty before class.

"We've got a horse now!" he said.

"A horse! Where?"

"In the garage, with a carriage. Dad drove out through it without noticing."

"Wow!" said Rusty. "What will that mouse think of next?"

"I don't know," said Alex grimly, "and what's more Carrie and I are beginning to think that he doesn't know himself. We think he's bitten off more than he can chew. He's certainly done it this time. We've got to get that horse out of there."

"Why," said Rusty. "Your dad's proved it doesn't interfere with his parking."

Alex passed a hand over his forehead. "But you can't just drive a car through a horse and carriage."

"You can if you can't see it," said Rusty reasonably.

But Alex felt that this was the last straw. He explained to Rusty his worries about how long the house and all its human and animal inhabitants might have been there. Rusty began to understand.

"And the Cedrics have disappeared," added Alex, "so I can't get the one who's doing all the damage to stop."

"Why don't you find out exactly how old the house is?" said Rusty. "Then at least you'd know what you were up against."

"How do I do it, though?" asked Alex.

"I dunno," said Rusty. "Why don't you ask Miss Henderson?"

This was one of Rusty's better ideas. Miss Henderson was assistant principal and very good with history. In fact she ran the local historical society. If anyone in town knew the age of his house, it would be Miss Henderson. As it turned out, she didn't, but she promised to find out and call him at home.

"I'm stopping in at the library on the way home anyway, so I can look it up for you," she said. What a nice boy, she thought to herself, a born historian.

Alex went home a little comforted but still nervous about what animal might materialize in their house next. At least whatever turns up won't be dangerous, he thought. I'm sure there weren't any wild animals in Victorian houses. But he was very wrong.

6

Space Invaders

By the end of the week there was still no sign of the Cedrics, and Alex didn't know how long he could conceal the empty cage from his mother. Dad was driving the car through the pony and carriage at least twice a day, and Mom said she could smell horse manure and he wasn't to bring bags of it home from the garden center in the car trunk. This made Dad angry, because he hadn't. And although Cedric had produced a pony, he hadn't finished with dogs yet. Alex never knew when another cold wet nose (that he knew wasn't really there) would press itself into his hand. It made him very jumpy. Cedric obviously wasn't going to stop without a very stern talking-to. And Alex couldn't give him that if he couldn't find him.

The only person who was really happy was Carrie. She glowed. Her life was full of cuddling, stroking, patting, and hugging, making up for nine lost years in one week, and all without a single wheeze. Every time Alex looked at her, his own worries lifted a little.

But he had been thinking a lot about the history of the house and how all these animals had belonged to real people who had moved on or were dead. And it made him feel very strange. Miss Henderson had discovered that the terrace had been completed in 1842. "Early Victorian," she said.

How many people have slept in this room in a hundred and fifty years? Alex wondered. Has anyone ever been born in here? Or worse, he suddenly thought, in all that time it was quite likely that someone had died in his bedroom! He prayed fervently that Cedric would stick to animal ghosts and not decide they needed more human company. And that was another thing—where was Cedric? And why had he disappeared at the very point when Alex had decided to ask him to stop?

"Mom," he asked in the morning, "what do you know about the people who lived here before us?"

"The Duggans?" she said. "Not much. They were an elderly couple who moved to a bungalow in the country to be near their daughter."

"No, not just the Duggans," said Alex. "I mean all the people who have lived in the house since it was built."

His mother laughed. "That's a bit of a tall order, Son. Why do you want to know?"

"It's for a project of mine," he said, carefully not mentioning the word "school."

"Oh, I see," said Mom, instantly taking

his request seriously, as he knew she would. "Well, you may be in luck, as it happens. When Dad was clearing out the attic, he found a whole lot of boxes of papers and photographs. I haven't had time to go through them yet, but they're in the spare room. You can rummage through them if you put everything back where you found it."

Alex cornered Carrie at the next opportunity, and they spent a couple of hours sifting through dusty documents and old photo albums in the spare room. Most of them dated back to the first owner, James Kinnear, who had been a colonel in the army in India. Carrie didn't like the sound of him very much; he had been a big game hunter as well as a soldier. There were old photos of tiger shoots and buck roasts, some showing a tall man with a black mustache and a gun. Colonel Kinnear had obviously been a busy man with lots of interests, one of which was photography.

And, Alex realized with a pang, the old colonel had been quite fond of animals when he wasn't killing or eating them. There were quite a few photographs of familiar dogs that were again roaming around the house.

Cedric must be nearly finished, thought Alex, with relief. Meanwhile, Carrie was growing more and more horrified with every photo she looked at.

"How could he?" she asked, her hands and hair streaked with dust. "How could he love his own pets so much and then go and shoot beautiful tigers?" Alex had no answer to that.

There were lots of photographs of the inside of the house too, and the children could recognize individual rooms under the clutter of potted plants and ornaments and heavy embossed wallpapers. The banisters and doors were all a dark varnished wood, not covered in white gloss paint as they were today.

The children got washed and went down to supper in a somber mood. On weekends the family always used the formal dining room. Mom said she spent enough time in the kitchen all week and didn't want to eat there too. Alex sat in his usual place with his back to the window and toyed with his meatloaf. All that talk about killing and eating animals had put him off meat a bit. He wondered whether to tell Mom that he was thinking of becoming a vegetarian. But a wise instinct advised him that in the middle of a meal she had just cooked was not the right time.

Bam! Bam! Two heads suddenly punched through the wall opposite him. First a black rhino with a single fearsome horn, then a glaring openmouthed tiger with its huge white teeth bared. Alex leapt to his feet with a strangled cry and raced out of the room. Heart pounding, he ran into the kitchen to see if the rest of the animals were on the other side of the wall. Thank goodness, there were no wrinkled gray rhinoceros legs on the kitchen counter or tiger-striped hindquarters with lashing tail on the electric stove. Alex quickly got a glass of water and went back.

"Sorry," he said, "something went down the wrong way."

But the heads were still there and although they looked very dead and detached,

he couldn't believe that Cedric was going to leave it at that.

"Carrie," hissed Alex, when he thought his parents weren't looking, and he tried to mime a tiger and rhino.

"Alex!" said Dad. "Stop making those terrible faces. Have you still got something stuck in your throat?"

Finally Carrie looked around and saw for herself. She turned pale. Both children were unusually helpful about taking the dirty dishes into the kitchen. Carrie quickly looked up at the wall just as Alex had done.

"They aren't all here—yet," he hissed. "But I think it's only a matter of time. What are we going to do with a full-size rhino and tiger to keep secret? Rusty will have a heart attack the next time he comes. We have to find Cedric. This has got to stop!"

Carrie nodded, her eyes as big as soup bowls. Supper seemed as if it would never end. But Alex remembered that there was a movie on television that his parents wanted to watch. And when he offered to make them some coffee and clean up too, they at last moved into the living room.

It seemed that the children were not the only ones waiting for that moment. Alex and Carrie were drying the dishes when they heard a bump at the kitchen door. It was pushed open by a long single horn. A real rhino would have been too wide for the doorway, but that didn't bother a ghost. It just surged through and stood looking at them. It took up an awful lot of kitchen. Silently Alex opened the door to the back-yard and it went out on its stately way. Then they both turned to look at the kitchen door again.

The face came very slowly around the door, long white whiskers first and then frilly cheek fur. It was a pretty beast, now that it was not snarling, and as tigers go, not particularly large. But its paws were huge and tawny, and its sinuous back and tail seemed to go on forever as it poured into the kitchen.

"That's better," said the tiger with a yawn and a stretch. "It's been a long time since I've been able to do that."

Surprisingly Alex and Carrie were not frightened, though a number of smaller animals could be heard scuttling into the hedges outside, and the Irish Guards had slunk out right after the rhino. The tiger blinked twice and stared at the children with an awful yellow blankness. "Care to tell me what's been going on?" he asked.

Alex didn't know where to begin and he felt it would be tactless to mention the colonel's hunting trophies. But after a while it was clear that it was all coming back to the tiger. And he didn't like what he remembered. He lashed his tail and coughed.

"Would you like to come for a ride?" he asked.

7

Enough Is Enough

If there is any experience in the world that can compare with riding a ghost tiger in the moonlight through the streets of your own town, it is hard to imagine what it could be. Alex and Carrie had waited until their parents had gone to bed before accepting the invitation. The tiger had joined the rhinoceros in the backyard until then. He was reluctant to come back into the house, so they led him out through the side gate by the garage. The pony whinnied uneasily as they went past.

The tiger padded down Ferry Road toward

town, carrying the children effortlessly on his muscular back.

"I can't believe this is happening," whispered Carrie. "It's just like one of those dreams where you can fly on something."

Alex nodded. "And just think," he said, "if anyone looked out of one of the houses, all they'd see would be us floating down the street about three feet off the ground!"

The tiger stalked on through the mild night, telling the children about his old home in the jungle in India. He never once mentioned the colonel.

"There's a tiger in the zoo," said Carrie before Alex could stop her. "It comes from Siberia."

The tiger stopped. "In the zoo? In a cage?"

"Well, it's not exactly a cage," said Alex, "more of a compound really. It has a lot of space."

"Does it have thirty square miles and a river?" asked the tiger.

"Er, no," said Alex.

"Then it is in a cage," the tiger replied quietly.

"But no one can hurt it where it is," said Carrie. "No one can come with guns and shoot it. And it doesn't have to hunt its own food."

"Perhaps I shall visit this tiger."

"We-ell," said Alex. "The zoo's quite a few miles out of town."

"Then I shall not do it tonight," said the tiger. "I had better take you back home or you will be tired in the morning."

The next morning Alex thought he might have dreamt it all, the glide through the quiet streets and the conversation with the tiger. Could he and Carrie have really done what they did, and totally without fear? He wanted to look at the old photographs again. He had a macabre urge to see if he could recognize their tiger from Colonel Kinnear's souvenir pictures and to see if there was one with the rhino.

Carrie wasn't allowed back into the spare room. Their last round of rummaging through all the dusty boxes had led to her first fit of sneezing since Cedric had entered the house. It didn't take Alex long to locate the right album, and he brought it out with him, first blowing the dust off its edges and thoughtfully wiping the cover with a clean handkerchief.

He and Carrie took it out into the yard to let the breeze blow away any remaining specks of dust. Carrie still looked dazed from their moonlight journey with the tiger, who was now lying camouflaged under the shadow of the sumac tree. The children sat with their backs to both tiger and rhino, which lay like a gray slab of stone where the rock garden should have been. They didn't want the animals to know they were looking at the pictures.

"Look, Alex!" Carrie cried suddenly.

"What? Where?" said Alex nervously.

"This photo. It's our hall, isn't it?"

"So what? You gave me an awful scare, yelling like that."

"Look at that, in the corner, by that funny old hatstand."

And then Alex saw what she meant. His blood ran cold. The colonel had an elephant's foot umbrella stand in the hall!

"No," he said. "You don't think . . . ?"

Carrie nodded. "If Cedric can do whole animals from just the heads, why not from the feet?"

"I can't cope, Carrie," said Alex desperately. "Not with a full-size elephant."

He had visions of coming home from school the next day and having to walk through an elephant before he could even get a snack.

Carrie stood up. "Come on," she said. "We've got to find Cedric."

"But we've looked everywhere," Alex objected.

"No we haven't," Carrie replied. "We haven't tried the attic."

Mungo Mackindoe was having a quiet Sunday morning with his books when there came a knock at his door. He bent down to open it and saw two upturned faces at the top of the ladder.

"Oh, hello, children," he said, surprised.

"We're looking for our mouse," said Alex.

"Are you really a magician?" asked Carrie at the same time.

Alex felt himself blushing to the tips of his ears the way he always did when Carrie said something he had been trying hard not to. But the boarder just smiled and said, "Come in," to Alex and, "I told your parents I was a logician," to Carrie. "You know, someone who teaches logic."

"Are you though?" persisted Carrie as they climbed in and looked around their own attic, which had somehow been transformed into a perfect place to do spells. The tasteful border of bats along the roof beams only added to the effect.

"I'm both, as a matter of fact," said Mungo. "I teach logic at the university. My magic I keep to myself."

"Cedric," gasped Alex, who suddenly caught sight of him peeping out of Mungo's breast pocket, then, to Carrie, "Oh, no, it's the wrong Cedric."

"Would you care to explain?" Mungo asked politely, offering them a seat. Alex

and Carrie found themselves telling him all about the two Cedrics and everything that had happened since Cedric the 55th had first materialized. The magician listened carefully. It was a relief to find a grown-up they could tell all this to who seemed as if he would understand.

"And now we're terrified that he's going to produce an elephant from the umbrella stand that used to be in the hall," finished Alex.

"So we've got to find him," said Carrie. "Have *you* seen him?"

"Oh yes," said Mungo, absentmindedly stroking his sandy whiskers. "I've seen him all right. He came back to me the night I moved in. I thought it was odd that he brought his grandfather with him."

The children gasped. "You mean you already *knew* Cedric?" asked Carrie.

"Of course," said Mungo. "He's my familiar."

8

~~~~~~

Stormy, With the Occasional Elephant

Alex swallowed a lump of something in his throat that tasted like jealousy.

"What's a familiar?" asked Carrie.

"All magicians and wizards have them," explained Mungo. "It's always an animal, though it can be any kind. They help us with our spells and," he added, "they sometimes get carried away and think they can do spells themselves."

"So Cedric hasn't really got magical powers at all?" asked Carrie. "Was he just using some of yours?"

"No," replied Mungo. "He can do some

simple magic. In fact, I'm rather impressed that he did as well as he did with this spell. But it's obviously gotten out of hand. I thought there was an odd atmosphere in this house—it felt sort of crowded for only four people—but I didn't know Cedric was involved. I should have guessed when he turned up."

"How did he come to be in the pet shop if he was your familiar?" asked Carrie. Alex hadn't said a word, ever since Mungo had said Cedric was his. "I lost him a few months ago, the last time I moved," explained Mungo. "Funny you should have given him his real name."

Alex thought, *I should have known it was too good to last. The only real pet I ever had and it turns out to belong to someone else! If only Cedric had been an ordinary mouse.*

"You don't really wish that, you know," said Mungo, looking at him not unkindly. "Now, let's get down to business. Our Cedric has decided to hide from me too. I think what we have here is a case of the sorcerer's apprentice."

Before he had time to relish that "our," Alex had a visual image of Mickey Mouse with a lot of brooms carrying buckets. The image was from a cartoon called *The Sorcerer's Apprentice*. It now seemed very significant that the cartoon had been about a mouse whose magic had gotten out of hand.

"You mean because he *can't* stop the spell?" Alex said. "We did wonder."

"Probably not," said Mungo.

"Then you'll have to stop it for him," said Carrie. "Or we'll get the elephant."

"It's not quite as simple as you suggest," said Mungo. "We do need Cedric to be around. I could do it on my own, by trial and error, but it would be a lot quicker with him, and we don't know how much time we've got."

Alex and Carrie came down from the attic to carry on the search, while Mungo made some preparations of his own. Although it seemed that the elephant was not going to be easily avoided, the prospect appeared much less daunting now that Mungo was involved. Alex felt a weight had lifted from his mind—something in the region of two tons.

There was a sort of brooding over the house, like a thunderstorm about to happen —or an elephant. The Brodie parents were jumpy. Alex and Carrie kept bumping into them as they looked in every cranny of the house for the real Cedric. Seamus and Fergus were restless too. They had never bothered much about the ghost cats, being the kind of dogs that believed in conserving their energy for when it was really needed, like for sleeping and digging holes. But now they were watching the black-and-white kitten very intently. And the kitten was stalking something down in the corner of the hall.

The Irish Guards barked; the kitten hissed;

the something turned out to be a very frightened Cedric. As the children ran into the hall, they spotted him right away. He was now sitting on the brass rim of an elephant's foot umbrella stand. It wasn't the kitten he was afraid of.

As if by magic, Mungo appeared in the hall too. "Cedric!" he said in a voice that contained reproof and relief in equal mouthfuls.

The little mouse looked apologetic. "I tried to stop it, I really did," he said. "I've been waiting for it here and trying to stave it off, but it's much too strong for me. This animal really wants to come back."

As he spoke, the umbrella stand began to quake and expand; the brass rim went zinging off it like an elastic band, catapulting Cedric through the air. Alex caught him in his left hand and solemnly passed him to Mungo. The children felt like bolting out of the hall. The very air was beginning to feel squeezed. But they couldn't because Mr. and Mrs. Brodie were coming into it from the kitchen.

"What's everyone doing out here?" asked Dad.

"Goodness, it's warm," said Mom, mopping her forehead. "There's probably going to be a terrible storm."

Then the children saw the impossible happen. The elephant's foot lifted up and came down, taking several steps toward them. It had been a front foot, as was obvious from the arrival of its partner and a matching pair of back feet, all three of which were now clearly visible. What joined them together was different from all the other ghosts. It was a hot mass of rage, a sense of a score unsettled by a magnificent lord of the jungle who had been butchered to make ornaments for a hunter's house. Mom and Dad couldn't see it, but with three other people who could, not to mention Cedric, the atmo-

sphere was so full of elephant-awareness that it was almost touchable.

Then Mungo reached out one hand and laid it on the elephant's trunk. With the other he made a sign in the air, and the hall erupted into a boiling kaleidoscope as lightning flashed through the stained glass in the door. Everyone's eyes were dazzled, and when they could see clearly again, the elephant had gone, taking all its feet with it. At that moment there was a huge clap of thunder right over the house. Or was it a trumpeting? Mungo's lips moved, but the children couldn't hear what he said.

"Phew," said Dad. "That was a close one!"

Alex soon realized with a pang that the Irish Guards had probably gone too, and the kitten. One look at Carrie showed that she was thinking the same thing. Mungo ceremoniously handed Cedric over to Alex.

"Your mouse, I believe, young man."

Alex held Cedric gently. Was this Mungo's way of punishing his apprentice? Had he taken Cedric's specialness away, so that he was now only fit for a life in a cage as a boy's pet? But as they all filed out of the suddenly very ordinary hall for an ordinary lunch, Mungo stayed back to whisper to the children. "There's no need for a familiar to live exclusively with its master. I take it I can borrow Cedric whenever I need him?"

Alex smiled happily. So did Cedric.

⌇

Mr. and Mrs. Brodie never understood how one minute Mungo Mackindoe was just a quiet boarder in the attic and the next he seemed to be their children's best friend. Alex and Carrie had immediately asked if they could take their lunch up to the attic and have it with Mungo. They even took their white mouse with them.

"Though what it was doing in the hall, I don't know," said Mom. "Alex didn't tell me it was lost."

"Well, count your blessings, Shirl," said Dad. "At least that Mackindoe doesn't seem to mind mice—or children for that matter. And it's better when everyone in a house gets along. Seems to me there's a better atmosphere in the place than there has been for days."

Cedric wouldn't have agreed with him. He was getting a good talking-to from Mungo for tampering with things he didn't understand.

"Oh, don't be too angry with him," pleaded Carrie. "He did it for me really, because I can't have real animals. It wasn't his fault that he couldn't stop."

"And we loved the animals," added Alex loyally, forgetting all the trouble the ghosts had caused. "It's just that there were a few too many."

"All right," said Mungo. "It could have been worse I suppose, particularly if you hadn't been so quick to realize that the elephant was coming."

"But Cedric," asked Carrie, "why did you run away?"

"And if you were going to run away to Mungo," said Alex, "why didn't you tell him you were in trouble?"

Cedric looked ashamed and embarrassed. He wasn't the proud and important mouse he had once been.

"I ran away because I thought you would guess I couldn't stop," he admitted. "I planned to tell Mungo the whole story, but then I got scared of what he might do to me." He hung his head. "I've been a foolish mouse. I thought I'd try and stop the elephant from coming, but I couldn't. And it nearly killed me."

He curled up pathetically on Carrie's lap and they all laughed.

"Let's hope you have learned your lesson then," said Mungo. "No more mouse magic!"

After eight days of miraculous animals, the house seemed strangely quiet that night. Alex stretched out luxuriously on his bed and yawned. He was looking forward to his first good night's sleep in over a week. He would miss the Irish Guards, and he knew that Carrie would be quietly crying into her pillow about Beauty, but it was wonderful not to have to worry about what creature would turn up next. And they still had a magician in the attic who could control lightning and unspook ghosts. Best of all, he still had Cedric. And all he had ever wanted was a pet of his own.

Cedric curled himself into a tight little ball and wrapped his long pink tail around his nose. He was tired. He had been tired for days, ever since he had stopped doing the spell and the spell had started doing him. Animal magic is hard work and elephant magic exhausting in proportion. He wasn't sure which had taken more out of him:

summoning the elephant or trying to prevent it. He would have a really good sleep. And tomorrow he would decide what to do to make the children's lives more exciting again. After all, he knew lots of other spells.